LESBIAN EROTICA HOT FRIEND COLLECTION BOOKS 1-2

Lesbian Office Romance:
Going Down During the Recession

Lesbians During the Pandemic:
Fun Lesbian Roommate Face Masks

AF507560

Brianna Bailey

CONTENTS

Title Page	1
Book 1	9
Book 2	17

BOOK 1

*Lesbian Office Romance:
Going Down During
the Recession*

Synopsis

The narrator, Sophia, is a well-educated brunette with pretty blue eyes. She worked at different industries after receiving her master's degree and ended up working one of New York's busiest financial stock brokerage offices.

The economy has entered a recession and she is laid off from her job along with her coworker, Jennifer.

Book 1

Lesbian Office Romance:

Going Down During
the Recession

The recession has hit the bottom of the market. Economic stock prices have dropped, and news websites and media have shown multiple companies going bankrupt. I was in my office when Jennifer looked at me in my eyes and said, "We're both laid off now." I looked at her and I said, "Let's go grab a couple of drinks after we pack everything up from our cubicles." We were both miserable with no job, no money, no assets.

We went to our favorite bar couple streets away from bustling Manhattan, New York with what was left in our credit cards. There were only a few people there because the recession caused everyone to just stay at home, but Jennifer and I needed to blow off some steam.

We needed to drink a little bit because we were just too stressed out from losing our jobs due to the markets crashing. I was constantly stressed every moment about my career and how I can get money to pay for bills. Having a therapeutic talking session with Jennifer was a good idea because we were both in the same industry. She was on the same page as me, we both had no income and we were both laid off.

Jennifer started loosening up after several cocktails. She bought us two more shots, "Here you go, cheers!"

I have always thought Jennifer's hair was always long, nice and wavy. Her beautiful eyes always had a strong stigma to it every time I walked past her down the halls of our stockbroker office, but I was no longer going to see her again now that we were laid off from our jobs.

Jennifer and I were both drinking away. I started to loosen up and began to forget about my stressful career. Jennifer held my hand and calmingly said, "It's going to be okay," and that's when she leaned in and kissed me.

Her lips were so soft, and I can feel her passion when she kissed me. I closed my eyes and the world just fell behind me, I forgot about the recession and began to relax. The comfort of her lips against mine made me just melt.

As Jennifer kissed me more, her tongue french kissed into my mouth with her tongue. She grabbed my hair with her hands, and I could feel her body against mine on the bar lounge chair.

I was worried the bartender was going to walk over to us and see everything, but no one bothered to look because everyone was so focused on their phones.

Jennifer grabbed my hand and we left the bar and we started to walk on the streets in a very zigzag direction. We got to the entrance of her apartment door and she grabbed her bright pink keys out of her pockets to get up to her apartment.

As we took the elevator up, we started making out against the elevator mirror wall. Her hips were pushed against mine and french kissed until the elevator doors opened on the 27th floor.

"This way," Jennifer grabbed my hand and we made our way through her apartment hallway and into her room where she had two bottles of champagne next to two glasses by the counter. She lit up a candle with an organic pinecone scent to it.

"Relax a bit tonight," Jennifer smiled. I replied, "What are we going to do about the stock market? We need to get a job and buy-in right now, we need to invest." Jennifer smiled and kissed me.

She popped the champagne bottles into our champagne glass. Before I could take a sip out of the champagne glass, Jennifer grabbed my hand and pulled me to her bed. She started kissing my neck and then she pushed me onto the bed.

Her hands unbuttoned each one of the buttons of my shirt and started to undress my shirt. As she caressed my hair with each kiss, she placed her comfortingly hands behind my lower back and the warmth of her hand felt so comfortable.

Jennifer took off her slip-on dress and her dress landed on the floor as she slipped it off. Her nipples were hard and pointy. She had no bra under her dress, and she stood there naked with her black thong lingerie and her stockings.

She took off her professional-looking framed glasses and put it on her bedside table and she leaned towards me to continue making out with me. I could feel her nipples against my breasts.

A giggled laugh came from her, "You like that huh?" I didn't say anything for a second and then I replied in a sexual enlightened manner, "Yes, keep kissing me." My pussy was wet at this point.

The scent of her hair smelled like lavender as I smelled her lovely presence with every kiss she made onto my neck. She kissed from my neck down to my nipples, then down to my stomach, and finally started licking my pussy.

My pussy was so wet, I wanted to orgasm with each tongue motion. My low back arched more as she stuck her tongue deeper into my vagina. Her hands started to fondle my breasts with each tongue lick on my clitoris.

I could feel her mouth inside of me. Her hands grabbed my breasts tighter as I moaned loudly to her tongue movements inside of my vagina.

My back arched again as the pleasure that I was feeling was so great. I yelled, "Don't stop, I'm coming." She squeezed my breasts harder with both her hands as I orgasmed with her tongue inside of me. There I laid on the bed with my former beautiful co-worker at the moment.

Jennifer and I both went on to our new jobs and new opportunities to survive the recession. I masturbate to her every time I think of her on my bed. I haven't seen her since that night but every time someone goes down on me, I dream of seeing her again.

BOOK 2

Lesbians During the Pandemic:
Fun Lesbian Roommate
Face Masks

Synopsis

The narrator, Sophia, is a well-educated brunette with pretty blue eyes. She studied Psychology in college and grew up in Orange County, California with two older sisters and a younger brother. Her favorite activities include paddle boarding and beach volleyball.

Book 2

Lesbians During the Pandemic:

Fun Lesbian Roommate
Face Masks

Everyone was ordered to stay home during the pandemic, and the state had ordered everyone to self-quarantine at home. I shared an apartment suite with my friend Victoria. She and I had picked up a bunch of groceries from our local farmers market before everyone was on lockdown.

Victoria had nice blonde hair and blue eyes. At this point, we were always both wearing face masks at home and we never left our apartment complex due to the lockdown of the pandemic.

Victoria was always nice and funny whenever I passed by her in the kitchen, but we were both adamant about always having our face masks on. I felt as if I was beginning to lose my social skills as this lockdown was beginning to take a toll on my interactions with people.

Victoria had a fun personality; she would some-times slap my ass in a fun way while I would be cooking in the kitchen. I kind of liked it every time she slapped my ass, I felt a bit aroused, but she didn't know I was into that kind of stuff.

It was Friday night and I had already finished my teleworking computer documents from my job in my room. I wanted to celebrate the weekend, but I couldn't go out and I was bored from staying at home all the time, so I pulled out the bottle of te-quila in my drawer and started taking shots.

I was feeling buzzed already, so I decided to turn on the music from my computer's speakers. I suddenly heard Victoria knocking on my door, I immediately put on my facemask and said, "Come in Victoria." Victoria saw my opened tequila bottle and she re-marked, "Oh you're a naughty girl drinking by your-self."

I put away my bottle and I was a bit shy from her re-mark, "No, it's not that. I'm just trying to celebrate the weekend, but I just can't go out because we are supposed to be in a locked down."

Victoria laughed, "You don't need to make excuses, I am a bit tipsy as well. I didn't need to work at all on my computer today."

The alcohol was starting to kick in, I looked into Victoria's beautiful blue eyes with the rest of her face covered by her face mask. The perfectly fit face mask complimented her face and it made her beautiful blue eyes stand out more.

Victoria was looking deep into my eyes as well; she leaned forward and tried to kiss my neck with her face mask in between her lips and my skin. Her face mask rubbed against my neck and my head tilted back as I felt the presence of her comfortable face next to mine.

I brushed her blonde hair with my right hand as she began to rub my neck with her covered face. Victoria's hands began to touch my lower back and that's when I started to get wet. I made a faint moaning sound as she caressed my neck up and down with her covered mouth.

Victoria firmly asserted, "Don't move, I'll be back in one second." I laid there on my bed with the door open thinking, "What is going on?"

Victoria quickly came back into my room but this time she was wearing a pink silk bathrobe. She leaned in again and started crossing my neck again and touching my lower back but this time her hands started to reach for my wet pussy.

She slipped her hands right into my pajama pants and into my panties, she slowly started fingering with her middle finger into my wet pussy. I finally whispered, "Yes, I love it."

My mind was filled with pleasure as she pushed me against my pillows on the far end of my bed and then used her to hands to pull off my pajama pants. I then took off my shirt and threw it to the floor. I had no bra on.

Victoria slipped out of her robe and then she stood there beautiful with her blonde hair, beautiful eyes, with her sexy pink facemask.

I looked down at her pussy and she was wearing a purple strap on dildo. Victoria stroked her purple strap on dildo with her two hands as if it was her dick and giggled.

I laid there on the bed looking at her beautiful figure as she climbed onto the bed. Victoria glanced at my pussy and said, "You're so wet." She spread my legs with her hands and then proceeded to rub my clitoris and then started to caress my hardened nipples with her face the texture of her face mask rubbing against my breasts was uniquely comfortable.

Victoria went and grabbed a bottle of lubricant from her robe pocket and squeezed it on her purple dildo. She stroked it a few times and slapped the tip of the dildo onto my clitoris and I moaned loudly as the dildo made a slapping noise against my clitoris.

I laid there in missionary position waiting for her to fuck me with her purple strap on dildo, "Victoria, give it to me. Fuck my pussy."

Victoria inserted her dildo into my pussy, and I screamed in excitement, "Yes, oh my god, yes." My pussy was so wet at this point, I wanted to orgasm.

Victoria then grabbed my nipples with her hands and at this point, my nipples were hard and pointy. The presence of her hand on my nipples while she fucked my pussy made me even wetter.

She then proceeded to thrust harder and harder into my pussy, I could feel her hands touching against me. I yelled, "I'm coming!" I orgasmed all over her purple dildo.

Victoria unstrapped her purple strap dildo and slid into the bed with me to cuddle. I wanted to do it again, but my body gave in and I was beyond tired from the sex.

Her nice slender body against my body was comfortable as we cuddled until we fell asleep. When I woke up, she was still laying there by my side.

This pandemic has caused a lot of inconveniences, but these experiences allowed me to get fucked in the pussy by Victoria. Getting fucked by Victoria was one of the most amazing experiences ever.

I hope you enjoyed this book.

Read these other awesome books by Brianna Bailey:

"My First Lesbian Encounter: Backdoor Rear Virgin Stretched"

Also check out other Brianna Bailey Books.

Sign up on the Fox & Bailey Awesome Book Club Online to receive updates on newly launched and recommended books!

Simply use this link: http://eepurl.com/gOEc29

Thank you for reading one of my books. I truly enjoyed writing this book and hoped you enjoyed reading this book. My passion for writing and sharing knowledge goes beyond the limit of the sky. Please leave me a 5-star review, it would truly help me immensely.

Thanks again!

9 798650 711995